Swan Publishing
Memphis, Tennessee

Copyright 2009
All Rights Reserved

ISBN 0-88144-410-3

Acknowledgments

To Mom,
Who I followed after
in writing and producing.

To Dad Jamison,
For being a part
of my life.

Contents

1	Captivated	3
2	The Beauty Factor	9
3	Unexpected Surprise	13
4	Who's The Man!	17
5	Where Good Girls Go Wrong	21
6	Too Close For Comfort	29
7	All Woman In Man's Clothes	35
8	All Honey Isn't Sweet	45

9	The Truth Be Known	49
10	Do The Seasons Change	61
11	The Better Man	67
12	Playing With My Mind	75
13	Hello Again	87
14	Make It Stop!	97
15	Only You, Lord	107

Beginning Prologue

The day was March twenty-fifth. You want to know how I remember so well? Because that's the day the sheriffs showed up at my house knocking on my door like they lost their minds. Well, here I go again for the third time in six months, another female trying to put a baby on me. But I'm not going down like that. I want a DNA test to prove my innocence. It's funny, when a brother has a little money, females will do just about anything to get a piece of his crop.

And so it was for Miss Sheila Anderson.

A good girl. Raised in church. Her father is the pastor of A.M.E. Baptist; but, even she is trying to get a B.M.W. these days. You know how it is, a black man working and all. But good girls go wrong.

See—I don't care anything about a female getting

Prelude to Dichotomy

pregnant. That's not my problem. She just has to be woman enough to handle her business and make that appointment. Then her problem won't have to be my problem.

Chapter One

Captivated

Now as Gabriel read the letter from Juvenile Court concerning Miss Anderson, his phone rang. He reached over to the voice of his partner Elmo who let him know that the Jones twins were in town and they all wanted to hook up "soon–like tonight." He agreed to swing by Elmo's place at around eight O'clock, sending word back to the twins to come with their best game hats on.

Handling legal matters at the courthouse worked up an appetite for lunch, so he stopped by a new Chinese restaurant which opened just blocks from his midtown penthouse.

Scoping the contemporary pink leather décor, an observing Gabriel sat down and picked

Prelude to Dichotomy

up a menu. Finally, I don't have to drive miles out of the way for a good plate of sweet-and-sour chicken, he thought. I could get used to this. With his head buried in the menu, her voice was as delightful as a hummingbird when she spoke over his left shoulder.

"Let me know when you're ready to order," said the waitress with her order slip ready.

Gabriel looked up at the lady in a pink silk dress.

"You're not Chinese," he said.

"Nor you," she acted surprised. "So, since we both realize we're non-Chinese, what can I get you?"

Gabriel chuckled. "Not only are you beautiful but you have a sense of humor."

"Thank you…Well, the House Special today is steamed vegetables with fried rice and sweet-and-sour chicken."

Gabriel felt lucky! "I'll have the House Special please, and throw in your phone number."

"I don't think my husband would like that," she answered.

Maybe not so lucky, he rethought, now

Captivated

noticing her princess cut diamond coupled with a wedding band. "Mm...You have one of those," said Gabriel.

"Yes, I have one of those." She jibed.

"Not good, well in that case let me give you my phone number."

"Why don't you just keep your number and I'll keep my husband," she said as she noted his order.

Gabriel, the King of Hearts leaned back and smiled at her a long moment. Inquisitively he posed, "If you don't mind me asking, how old are you?"

"Has anyone ever told you that it was rude to ask a woman her age?"

"I think my momma may have told me a time or two."

The woman looked at Gabriel who was as charming as they come. "What difference will it make?"

"I believe it will make my visit at this fine establishment worth it," he said smoothly.

"Mister, has anyone ever told you that you were full of it?" Replied the waitress, thinking

Prelude to Dichotomy

that this overly confident man may have been her most obnoxious customer yet.

"Yes ma'am, a time or two," he laughed.

As Gabriel sat in his 128i black convertible that evening waiting on Elmo, a man and woman passed by his vehicle kissing and holding hands.

He thought about the lady he met earlier that day at the Chinese restaurant. How committed she seemed to be to her husband; he shook his head.

If I couldn't steal her heart for at least one second, she must really love her man. Just then Elmo climbed in the car catching Gabriel musing; he noticed that his partner wasn't up to his usual self tonight. "What's up with that look on your face?"

"I'm good rogue, I was just thinking about a female I met earlier today."

"She must be something if she has your mind in the loop."

Man, I couldn't crack the code."

"Quit lying dog, you?" Elmo answered incredulously at his idol who was a natural born pro at scoring with women; he could easily slide

Captivated

into home base or foul out of any relationship in one quick inning.

"I can't believe it myself. She was a piece of work bro, you should have seen her," Gabriel said while shaking his head.

"Let's put all of that aside," said Elmo, attempting to retract his partner to the date at hand. "I know one code you're going to be able to crack and if my memory serves me right you've been wanting to crack it for a long time."

"Sure you're right!"

Gabriel and Elmo gave each other dap. As the two were on their way to visit the Jones girls, Gabriel unsuccessfully attempted to erase the former lady's impression from his mind; and though he realized she was married and clearly committed to her husband, he desired to see her again.

Chapter Two

The Beauty Factor

As the two players of the evening entertained the Jones twins, Gabriel realized it had been a couple of years since he had seen them and was a little upset, being Elmo neglected to tell him that the twins went from petite to queen plus; and he took the first opportunity to express his displeasure to Elmo, as soon as he saw the two thoroughly engaged in feminine chatter.

"So what do you think about the girls?" Elmo asked low toned.

"You should have told me they gained weight,"

Gabriel answered in the same manner.

"My brother, think of it this way, you have more territory to cover," his friend replied, not

Prelude to Dichotomy

seeing an issue.

"Mo, you know you're wrong. There's only one thing I like big on a woman and that's her bank account."

"What are you two fine gentlemen over there whispering about?" Rhonda interrupted.

"I was just telling Gabriel how fortunate we are to be in the company of two gorgeous women," answered Elmo.

Gabriel looked sharply at Elmo as if one look could have shred him to pieces.

"And how do you like what you see?" Rhonda asked, seeking Gabriel's approval.

"Well the jury is still out," said Gabriel.

Elmo choked on his drink and interjected, "What my friend is trying to say is–"

"I know what I mean," retorted Gabriel.

Elmo nudged Gabriel's knee under the table to shut him up.

Gabriel cleared his voice and humbly retracted his statement, "What I mean is–the jury is still out due to the beauty factor."

"And what is that?" Quizzed Tonya.

"The beauty factor is when a woman's

The Beauty Factor

beauty is so off the chart that it takes a special jury to rule on her behalf."

"Girl, I'm getting hot up in here!" Tonya fanned herself and turned to her sister.

Good save, thought Elmo, forcing down his drink.

About a minute later Gabriel looked across the table to see Rhonda sumptuously licking the barbecue sauce off her hands, finger-by-finger, which proved to be more than his ego could take for one night.

"Excuse me young lady, would you like some more food? I mean, it's no problem…I could order you another plate of those ribs–"

"No, I'm fine" said Rhonda, attempting to ignore the insult.

"Oh," Gabriel continued to be an unrestrained jerk at his best, "the way you were licking all ten, I thought you may have wanted a second or maybe a third helping."

"What are you trying to say about my sister!" Defended Tonya.

"I'm not trying to say anything, what I am saying is that it looks like her big behind is either

Prelude to Dichotomy

hungry or she wasn't paying attention in kindergarten; I don't know…But she and her fingers over there most definitely have a thing going on."

Rhonda and Tonya looked at each other and began cursing at Gabriel. Immediately, he stood up and took out a hundred dollar bill. He laid it on the table, turned to his buddy then said, "Listen man, I'm not feeling these quarterbacks, here's some money and here are the keys to my car. Pick me up in the morning and don't be late." Gabriel walked away from the table leaving the two angrily aroused ladies, while Elmo followed him outside.

"Gabe, you don't know what you're going to miss."

"Look at it this way, you have two of them to play with now," said Gabriel. So he turned, climbed into a taxi, and it drove off.

Chapter Three

Unexpected Surprise

A week and a half had passed since that unforgettable night with the Jones girls. Thank God for beautiful women! Gabriel recollected, as he was now at his office desk finishing the last details of a jingle contract.

His secretary called to inform him that Mr. Davis wanted to see him right away. The CEO of Prolific Artists Production & Marketing had hired Gabriel five years ago as a music producer over the department of commercial business. Having much respect for his boss, Gabriel swiftly collected himself and made his way to Mr. D's spot.

"You needed to see me, Sir?"

"Yes, come in Gabriel and please, have a

Prelude to Dichotomy

seat."

"Thank you," he answered, leaving the door opened.

"Gabriel, I have a close acquaintance who just moved into the state. She and her husband have quite the knack for investing. They have bought several chains in the city and I volunteered your professional expertise."

"What type of chains are they?" Gabriel questioned, sitting far back in his seat.

"They bought Ballard's Barbecue House and two Oriental restaurants...Speaking of my little Angel–" At that moment the boss stopped and shifted his attention to the gorgeous woman. Dressed in a white Italian designed blouse, a gray knee length business skirt with charcoal high heels, she entered the room right past Gabriel into Mr. Davis' welcoming arms. Gabriel's mouth dropped and he shifted to the edge of his seat, being caught by sheer surprise at her familiar face. He listened as Mr. D. finished his introduction. "Here she is," Mr. D. proclaimed adoringly. "Rachel, I would like you to meet Gabriel, my right hand man."

Unexpected Surprise

Rachel turned to Gabriel and looked. She was as equally shocked to see him again. It took ten seconds for the wise man to catch the apparent wave of intensity between the two of them.

"Is everything alright Rachel?" The old man inquired.

"This gentleman and I have already met," she sounded like a frog had just jumped into her throat.

"I hope it was a good meeting," he addressed them both.

"Let's just say it was a Grande Memphis welcome," she replied, glancing over at Gabriel.

"Mr. Davis, if I would have known that this young lady was connected to you in any way, I'd never have asked her out on a date," Gabriel replied innocently.

Mr. Davis was amused and turned to Rachel, "So, how was his pick up line?"

"Like something from Memphis," she answered wittingly, "a little dusty."

They all started laughing.

Then Gabriel offered his hand and asked in his most formal manner, "Can we start over? Hi,

Prelude to Dichotomy

I'm Gabriel Armour, it's nice to meet you."

Rachel looked into Gabriel's warm and handsome smile as if she had seen a cunning anaconda and hesitantly responded to his introduction with a firm right handshake. "I'm Rachel O'donald, I'll let you know if it's a pleasure after I've gotten to know you better."

Gabriel looked over at Mr. Davis and spoke defensively, "Mr. D., I don't think she's going to give me a break."

"Oh, I think she has you pegged accurately enough. If she knows what's best for her, she would keep her guards up." Mr. Davis gestured in boxing form toward Gabriel, and smiled at Rachel, then ending the conference, said "Well, I'm going to let you go with Gabriel and you tell him what you need; he's the best I've seen. I can guarantee you will be satisfied with the jingles he creates for your business."

Rachel hugged Mr. Davis and thanked him for everything. Then she and Gabriel left Mr. Davis' office to discuss the details of her their dealings.

Chapter Four

Who's The Man!

It was a lovely evening and the stars danced amid the velvety blue sky. Gabriel sat with a typical Friday night 'prize' on the veranda of a dinner cruise boat called The Queen III. As he and she gazed romantically on the panoramic view, he glanced across the balcony and captured Rachel with a gentleman overlooking the river and rapidly moving toward his table. The tall, distinguished man who firmly held her waste was obviously the enraptured husband.

"Mr. Armour, how are you doing this evening?"

"I'm doing well," Gabriel acknowledged Rachel.

"Robert, this is Gabriel Armour. He's the

Prelude to Dichotomy

one who Uncle Edward has working on our promo package," Rachel said, in a referring manner.

Robert and Gabriel extended hands cordially.

"It's really a pleasure to meet you," Gabriel spoke.

"Likewise, I've heard nothing but good things about you," Robert replied.

"Thank you. I hope you have been satisfied with my work," Gabriel added.

"You're a genius," Robert complimented. "It's amazing to me how a person can take someone's thoughts and bring them to life the way you have."

"I'm glad you're pleased...I'm sorry you two, this is my lovely date Julia," he pointed out. "Julia, these are The O'donalds. I'm doing some work for them."

Julia mannerly greeted The O'donalds.

"Excuse me," said Rachel mindfully, "aren't you Miss Tennessee?"

"Yes," replied Julia.

"You are so beautiful."

Who's The Man!

"Thank you."
"Well, we're not going to detain you two any longer," ended Robert, "Enjoy your meal."
"Likewise," said Gabriel, as he and his prized companion carried on into the evening.

Chapter Five

Where Good Girls Go Wrong

Monday morning Gabriel arrived at work early when a young lady stormed in.

"Mr. Armour, I tried to stop her–" explained the secretary, "but she just ran right past me."

"It's alright Sara, but stay close just in case we need to call the boys," he answered.

"Yes Sir," His secretary complied.

"Why haven't you returned my calls?" said Sheila, who saw by now that she had only been a sweet and tasty appetizer, and there was little she could do about it. Still, maybe he was only hiding his feelings and in seeing her again his affections would be rekindled.

Prelude to Dichotomy

"I've been too busy," he answered carelessly.
"It's funny, you weren't saying that when you were on top of me," she retorted.
Thinking he should have taken his unscrupulous friend Elmo's advice more seriously, who told him to be careful how he treated God's women, Gabriel replied with a brief pause of guilt. "O.K., and what's your point?" Then, quickly dismissing the feeling he added, "That was then and this is now." "What are you going to do about your baby I'm carrying?" Persisted Sheila, a little louder and clearer now as if Gabriel had a hearing problem.
Gabriel calmly stood and walked over to his office door to close it. "You need to lower you voice.

Anyway, I won't know it's mine until I get a DNA test; and to be honest, I'm hoping that it doesn't have to go that far."
You're the only person I've ever been with," she answered. Her journal marked March twenty-fifth of last year as the day she had given him her virginity.
"Girl, if you knew how many females this

year alone have quoted that line to me, it would blow your mind." He thought about the last girl he hooked who promised to curse him with voodoo. Sheila angrily picked up a silver vase sitting on his desk and threw it at Gabriel, barely missing his head. He instinctively shifted his head to the left from the speedy object, "You need to cool yourself down."

Defeated, she dropped in a chair and quietly cried in front of his desk. Gabriel also sat down at which time he opened his desk drawer and took out a checkbook. Glancing over at her, as if to quickly assess her worth, he began to fill the check out. Afterward, he slid the signed paper across his desk. She looked over at the check which read, payable to the order of Sheila Anderson for the amount of five hundred dollars.

So, this is how it goes, the church girl mindfully reflected. She had been trusting and naïve; he had been deceitful and clever. She read his heartbeat, or so it seemed; he read her innocence well and banked on it. Blown away by appearances, she mistook good character for good attributes. Forsaking her values, she had settled

Prelude to Dichotomy

for a well-wrapped package who was blessed with good looks, intelligence and charm but who lacked the essential elements of the heart. A shrewd and conformed Gabriel was her introduction to the world. A world this good girl was not prepared for. She wiped the slowly fallen tears on her sleeve then picked up the check. Suddenly, it felt like she had grown taller. Regaining her composure, she stood and with one last heartbroken glance at him, exited the room.

Gabriel sat in his office trying to make sense of what went down when there was a knock at his door.

"Is everything alright Gabriel?" Asked his boss.

"Yes Sir," answered Gabriel, collectively.

"May I come in for a couple of minutes?"

"Yes, come in."

Mr. Davis walked directly in front him.

I'm sorry for my friend's outburst," Gabriel began.

"Is she going to be alright?"

"Yes Sir."

"Someone you're dating?" His employer further inquired.

"No Sir, it's over between us," he assured, sliding the checkbook into his desk.

Mr. Davis stood looking at Gabriel; now deciding to express his prolonged concern for the promising young man who reminded him so much of himself, when he was wild and living life on the edge. "Do you mind if I tell you a story?"

Gabriel braced himself for the lecture.

As he walked over to the glass window, Mr. D. gently spoke. "Over thirty-two years ago, there was a very special lady in my life. She was madly in love with me and I was madly in love with myself. She was what the old fellows called 'the cream of the crop.' Because of my old ways, gambling and entertaining many, many lovely women, she became weary and finally gave me an ultimatum. It was going to be 'her–and only her–or my freedom.'" He hesitated and stated regretfully, "Son, I stand before you thirty-two years later still haunted by my bad decisions."

He cleared his throat. "Gabriel, if you don't remember anything I've said, remember that

Prelude to Dichotomy

good looks, money, and all the pleasures of women will only carry you so far before you become faced with a sad awakening; in time, you'll realize you're all alone".

"So Mr. D., what happened to her?" Gabriel prodded, curious to know how this old man's love story ended.

Mr. Davis turned his back against the glass window as he reminisced. "She saw that I wasn't going to change, and to be honest, I didn't think she would leave me, but she fooled me…Yes, she fooled me big time. Eventually she married a fellow in the Army who was a good guy. He did love her royally. I was fortunate enough to hold onto one part of her, our friendship. Her family and I grew closely; if you saw them, you saw me. We even took trips together."

"I'll bet that was awkward," Gabriel interjected.

Mr. D. looked at Gabriel now. "It started out that way, but over the years they became my family; all I had left. I was honored when they asked me to be their child's God parent. You've met Mrs. O'Donald."

Where Good Girls Go Wrong

"You're telling me that Rachel is your God daughter? It was her mother? That's some wild stuff, Mr. D., was she still in love with you?"

"Yes, she was, but we kept it between us and we made sure we didn't cross any lines. I had to man up and realize that I had my time and I didn't use it wisely, so it wouldn't have been right for me to make waves in her happy home. I settled for being able to love her from afar."

Mr. Davis had unveiled his story to Gabriel and while he now stood leaning on the door he added, "Son, I hope you're hearing what I'm saying."

Chapter Six

Too Close For Comfort

Autumn came in fully with its multi-colored leaves spreading over the sidewalks to be swept up by its gusty high winds. The O'donalds came in fully expecting an effective and efficient commercial package to be laid out by their favorite business associate Mr. Armour.

"Good morning," Gabriel greeted the two.

"I don't know if I should say good morning or if I want my fifty back after the way you whipped on me at the golf course yesterday," Robert replied.

Gabriel and the O'donalds laughed.

"I heard you were a master on the golf course," said Rachel.

"I'm alright. Believe it or not, Mr. D. whips

Prelude to Dichotomy

on me".

"So you had to take it out on me!" Robert jested.

They all laughed.

"Please, you two have a seat. I have your disk right here. He removed it from under several manila folders.

I see they've been keeping you busy," said Rachel.

"Ghh-yes," he confirmed with a facial gesture. "I just took off a week and look what I've come back to."

"Look at it this way, when you're good–you're the man," said Robert.

"Speaking of being the man, Lacy told me that the two of you spent the weekend on your brand new boat," teased Rachel.

"That's one of the problems with dating among friends, they don't keep secrets," smirked Gabriel.

"Not only that Mr. Armour, you're making it hard for the next brother. My wife is trying to get me to buy one of those fancy boats now."

Gabriel looked over at Rachel. "Rachel, are

Too Close For Comfort

you pestering my good friend?"

"I don't think of it as pestering, I just want him to take vacations so we can do things together besides work. It's not like he can't afford it. Gabriel, you know my husband is a workaholic," she justified.

"Well on that note, I can't say anything. I'm in the same boat as your husband."

Rachel looked intently over at her husband with her entrancing, slanted brown eyes which could make any man melt.

"Now Gabriel, I know you just saw her put that eye action on me," Robert said playfully.

Gabriel coughed and straightened his tie jokingly, "I thought I might need to excuse myself for a moment."

"Funny, really funny," said Rachel sarcastically.

The O'donalds continued talking with their newfound friend Gabriel and enjoying his company. He eventually came around to letting them hear the music for their next line of commercials which they found very satisfactory; and once again, he was the hero who saved the day.

Mid-Chapter Prologue

Talk about crazy! The way it all went down... This is the one time I got myself knee deep in the wild. It was one of those reckless dilemmas. I mean, I've been in some sticky situations, but I think I can definitely pinpoint this as the stupidest thing I've ever done.

Chapter Seven

All Woman In Man's Clothes

It was a mad, stormy night in April when Gabriel was at home and his phone rang. "Hey Girl," he answered coolly, thinking it was his companion calling to cancel their date for the evening.

"Gabriel, I'm sorry to bother you, but Robert asked me to call since I'm not too far from your house," Rachel sounded frustrated.

"It's no problem, what's going on?" He spoke back.

"I'm stuck out in the rain, I have a flat," she answered.

"Where are you exactly?"

"I'm down from the restaurant in front of

Prelude to Dichotomy

GeeGee's.

"Keep your doors locked, I'm on my way." Gabriel grabbed his keys, as he was familiar with the all-night bar she mentioned. He quickly phoned his female friend to postpone and turned the oven off, leaving the steamy hot serving for two. As he listened to the radio on his way, the weather man reported a tornado warning located in their vicinity. Gabriel figured it would be safer to pick Rachel up and take her back to his house until the storm had passed...Safer from the tornado, anyway!

But the storm that had been stirring inside him every time he was around her, he wasn't too sure about.

From the first day he saw her in the restaurant it seemed she awakened something in him that he didn't know he had; a conscience. He had resolved to maintaining a 'professional only' relationship with her, except months of business deals made it harder for him to get her out of his head. He knew women, but she intrigued him like no one else had, and even fewer had denied him. Gabriel was not a man acquainted with re-

All Woman In Man's Clothes

jection.

He arrived at the scene of a drenching wet and muddy woman quickly loading tools in her trunk, apparently unsuccessful at the attempt of fixing the flat. He jumped out to help and they drove back under a marbled gray sky, listening to the crackling of thunder.

Now safely back at his house, he offered her a loan of dry clothes and his laundry room of which she gratefully accepted.

"I hope I didn't disturb you. I see you have an elegant table arrangement with two place settings," she said as they passed the dining room.

"No, you're fine. I should be thanking you for calling, I was a little tired anyway. I need to stop entertaining during weekdays."

"I sure appreciate you coming to get me," she stated, feeling certain she had infringed upon his single space.

"It truly was no problem," he reassured. "Follow me, I have some clothes in the guest room if you don't mind wearing men's clothes."

"No, I don't mind as long as I'm dry."

Gabriel grabbed some clothes in the room

Prelude to Dichotomy

from the first drawer he saw; his mind had started to malfunction as she stood in the room with him. Something about this woman caused crazy ideas to whirl through his head. *Danger zone*. He sensed a meltdown. Being this vulnerable to any woman was scary, but he found the sensation of being around her was too wonderful to refuse. This is totally against the rule, he reasoned. Every man knows the 'buddy rule.' You don't mess with your buddy's girl—or in this case your buddy's wife. It's just not kool. But his heart betrayed his dating ethics as he stood there longing to undress her. He quickly handed her a T-shirt and some pants then walked away. Through the short hallway, he shook off the lustful tugging. *If only for one night we could be intimate.* As soon as the thought came, he ignored it.

He knew his boundaries.

"Have you had dinner"? He shouted from the kitchen.

"No, I haven't", she called back.

"Would you like to try your luck at Cafe Armo'r?"

"Sure. I'll be right out." She finished rolling

All Woman In Man's Clothes

up the baggy legged pants and walked barefoot toward the front. Gabriel put the lobster entrée on their plates as Rachel took a seat at the table.

"Everything smells so good, where did you learn to cook?"

"Believe it or not, I learned from my father. As a boy, he used to always tell me that a man should know how to do three things; cook, clean, and hem his own clothes. Just in case a fellow couldn't get his woman to do it for him, he wouldn't be out in the cold."

"It seems as if he gave you some well taken advice," admired Rachel.

Gabriel reached over and took the white wine out of the ice bucket. "Would you like a little?"

"Just a little," she said, using her fingers to describe precisely what she meant.

The setting was warm and riskily romantic. Gabriel had just the day before purchased a jazz CD of the latest love kicks and had left the soft music playing to a gas fireplace of burning amber coals. As they ate and talked, Rachel enjoyed the change of atmosphere compared to the threaten-

Prelude to Dichotomy

ing storm they had just come out of.

She pushed up her oversized sleeves and turned her red lips around the gold trimmed crystal.

You may be dressed in men's clothes, but you are all woman, his thoughts ran.

"Do you always go all out for your dates? I mean, fireplace and roses…Inquiring minds want to know," she asked curiously.

"I look at it this way, why not make a woman feel like a princess? I know every woman wants to feel special once in her life, even if it is only for one night."

Looking at him intensively, she evaluated, "I can see why the ladies are crazy about you, you're charming and gifted with words."

Gabriel laughed at her observation.

"What about love, Gabriel?" She posed seriously.

"Truth?" Asked Gabriel.

"Truth," she shot back.

"Sometimes I wonder if I will ever fall in love, but I'm pretty satisfied with my life as it is. Anyway, everybody isn't as fortunate as

All Woman In Man's Clothes

Robert."

Rachel glanced at Gabriel and he glanced back.

"I look at it this way, everybody isn't meant to be married", he shrugged dismissingly.

"Tell me you're not lonely," she probed.

Gabriel leaned back in his seat and took a deep breath, "O.K. Doctor Phil, I'm sometimes lonely.

Have you ever thought about being a psychiatrist?"

"No, but I just might after tonight."

"You are truly something, woman," he spoke while thinking, *I wish she was mine*.

Gabriel arose from the table and walked onto his back deck. He looked out into the rain storm. It was nine sixteen. "What would you like to do? It doesn't look like the storm is letting up. If you want, we'll give it more time, and when it's over I'll take you to your car and change your tire."

She agreed, now exhausted. He pulled extra covers from the guest room closet and laid them down on a chair. Afterward, he returned to his own bedroom.

Prelude to Dichotomy

Well into the night had passed. The storm seemed to be as endless as the sea. Now, at one O'clock in the morning, Gabriel was awakened by the sound of a television. He grabbed a robe, threw it over his bare back and shorts, then went into the front room. Rachel was sitting on the sofa with a thick, brown camping cover over her legs.

"Hey, is everything alright?" He asked.

"I'm fine, I just couldn't sleep. I hope I didn't wake you."

"No, I'm good. Do you mind if I have a seat?"

She patted the couch as a gesture for him to sit down beside her.

"I forgot you were even here, I thought my television came on by itself," he admitted.

"I was checking to see what the weather forecast is saying. I think I may be stuck until the morning, if you don't mind."

"It's kool, I don't have to be at work until ten O'clock." Gabriel laid his head on the sofa pillow and was again fast asleep.

It happened during the course of dawn.

All Woman In Man's Clothes

How she found herself into his arms seemed mysterious. They awoke at the same time. Gabriel opened his eyes looking into hers. They stared. The longer they stared, the faster the gulf between them closed…Until they found themselves in a world where there was no one but them, and nothing else mattered but the sweet intimacy they shared at that moment.

Chapter Eight

All Honey Isn't Sweet

Gabriel was preparing for a meeting with the board that Wednesday, when Mr. Davis came in first and sat at the end of the conference table.

"So are you going to say something?" Asked Gabriel.

"Son, I have a proposition for you."

"O.K.. Let me hear it."

"You know next week is going to be Mable's last week. I want you to take her job as the media director. I know you turned it down before, but you're the man for the job," reasoned Mr. Davis.

"I understand you have a lot on your plate, but listen, I think you can handle it. I'm not going to take no for an answer. I wouldn't feel right giving someone else a twenty-five thousand dol-

Prelude to Dichotomy

lar raise when you've been filling in for the job anyway."

"Since when did her position offer a twenty-five thousand increase?"

"Listen son, it doesn't go with the package, but because I want you to have it, I'm making it available to you and only you. So what do you say?"

"Can I have her old office?"

"Only if it will convince you to say yes."

Gabriel walked in front of Mr. Davis, "Thank you sir, for the chance."

"Well, I'll need to break the news to the others who applied for the position," he added.

Gabriel paused curiously, "but sir, I didn't apply for the position."

"You know it, and I know it. Let's make it our little secret," smiled Mr. Davis.

Gabriel nodded his head as everyone began to fill the room. With one last remark, Mr. Davis remembered a message for Gabriel and innocently becoming liaison to the affair, "I almost forgot, Mrs. O'donald asked me to have you call her."

All Honey Isn't Sweet

She had asked Gabriel to meet her. He suggested that the riverfront at noon would be a good place and time. Gabriel waited several minutes on a bench until Rachel arrived and sat beside him.

"Sorry I'm late, I was hung up in traffic, so, how have you been?" She said, attempting to sound aloof.

"I'm alright."

After a long silence, Rachel took a deep breath. "Gabriel what happened between us should have never happened."

He looked out at the river, then over at Rachel. "You're right, it shouldn't have happened, but it did. If I could speak freely, since that unfortunate but yet lovely evening, I've had nothing else on my mind but you, and I know it's wrong—"

Rachel interrupted, "Gabriel, we can't let it happen again. There's a lot more wrong that can come out of our bad decision than you know."

"For the record lady, something is going on inside me I can't explain."

Rachel put her head down in her hands try-

Prelude to Dichotomy

ing not to let Gabriel know that there were demons on her back as well. "We can't do this again, Gabriel."

"Tell me something, I know you regret it, but if you weren't married where would we stand? I mean, a lot happened that morning, and I think you remember the things that were said between us; I meant ever word."

Rachel stood to walk away when she stopped and broke down crying. He walked behind her and turned her to him and held her.

So, Gabriel and Rachel vowed not to ever do what they had done again. But a vow is only as powerful as the soul, and they found not the strength. Caught up over and again, each ran into the arms of the forbidden; his friend's wife and her adulteress lover.

Chapter Nine

The Truth Be Known

Rachel walked into her house after a long and busy day. The place smelled like a New York Italian restaurant. One of which she and Robert had not visited together in a long time, since their own climbing success in the restaurant business. In fact, much of their time together had been sacrificed these days, as Robert's frequent travels out of town had required it. She peeked into the kitchen to find her husband sporting a chef hat. He walked over to unarm her of her clothing.

"How's my love doing this evening?"

"I'm doing good, just a little tired," she answered. Robert slipped his hand around her and pulled her to him. He tenderly kissed her lips. "You know baby, a man can tell a lot by

Prelude to Dichotomy

a woman's kiss, and your lips are telling me that you have a lot on your mind," he said concerned.

"I'm sorry, let me go freshen up and I'll probably feel a lot better. What's the occasion?"

"Well, if you feel you need one, how about because I'm mad about you."

Rachel looked at him with a thoughtful smile,

"Thank you for loving me, my husband." She made her way up the stairs through their bedroom into their sunken tub to find it filled with pink bath bubbles and red rose peddles. How mindful Robert had been of the little things. He had been good to her.

Dear God, what's wrong with me? She leaned her head back against the tub and closed her eyes, thinking. Soon, she released her problems to the waves of the water.

Robert came in to find his wife passed out in the bath tub. He reached in and lifted her wet body out of the water and carried her to a chaise in their bedroom; wiping her off, she began to stir. He left her to change into a lounge pants suit and five minutes later she made her way down

The Truth Be Known

the stairs.

During dinner, Robert suggested she get away to rest at their cabin for the weekend, since he would be leaving Friday afternoon. She decided to take his advice.

The weekend came fast. Even though the trip to the cabin only took an hour and forty-five minutes, it seemed much further from the stirring city. When her cell phone rang, her gut feeling told her to ignore it. "Hello".

It was Gabriel. "Can you talk?"

"Yes, How are you?"

"I'm good, I haven't seen you in a couple of days and I was just making sure you were doing alright."

"I'm fine. I'm just catching up on some needed rest."

"That sounds like something I need to be doing, but maybe next weekend when I get back in town."

"Where are you?" She asked inquisitively.

"I'm in Nashville. I got a hold of some preseason tickets to the football game," said the sports lover.

Prelude to Dichotomy

"Stop playing."
"Why do you say that?"
"Have you spoken with Robert this week?" She asked.
"No, why?"
"I'm spending the weekend at our cabin, it's right outside Nashville."
"Is he with you?"
"No, he's in Los Angeles for the weekend."
"How strange is that?"

She wondered the same thing. This had not been the first time nor the second, that convenience seemed to have thrown them into their present circumstance.

"Would you like some company?"
"No. We may need to keep our distance. You just enjoy the game," she suggested.
"Well, if you need me call me and I'll be there."

As Gabriel and Rachel carried on with light conversation it became harder for them to cut off.

"Well, let me get off the ringer", he finally stated.

The Truth Be Known

"Yes, come."

Silence.

"So, you want me to come and keep you company?"

"Yes, hurry before I change my mind."

When Rachel saw Gabriel's car pull up the winding drive, she went out to meet him, asking if he had any problems finding the cabin because it took so long. He was as impatient to see her and grabbed her, barely out of the car himself.

"No, you gave me pretty good directions," he answered and smiled at her.

"It's good to see you."

"You too," she said, wrapping her arms around him.

"I like your get up." He referred to her pink striped short set that fit her extra nicely, as he followed her into the cabin.

Rachel glanced at him as to imply, don't say another word. She handed him a soda at the kitchen bar and they sat.

"So, how long is Robert going to be out of town this time?"

"Sunday, and how long are you going to be

Prelude to Dichotomy

in Nashville?"

"I'm going to be leaving after the game. Would you like to go?"

"Sorry, I'm not a football fan. I'm going to hang out here at the cabin."

"May I look around?" He asked, following the well designed architecture.

"Feel free."

"This is a beautiful place you have here. Your husband has good taste," Gabriel noted the classic art collectibles cascading along the high beams.

Rachel nodded in agreement.

"I've never seen a pool that overlooked a lake," he stated, impressed.

"Robert's father had this house custom built; it's been selected a model for several magazines.

"Yes, I can believe it. He did a great job."

As he passed in front of her, she took in his cologne.

"You smell nice," she complimented.

"Thank you. I think you smell nice too."

They both laughed, behaving like it was their first love. Rachel got up and took Gabriel by the

The Truth Be Known

hand, leading him outside and down a path.

"Where are you taking me?" Feeling a sudden fear, as his memory flashed before him of the many females he victimized, he joked nervously, "you're not taking me to do me in, are you, ha ha."

"Just walk!"

There, through some high bushes, they stopped. The sight was breathtaking; thousands of white butterflies flying everywhere. For every summer flower in an endless field, there was a beautiful albino butterfly gracing its presence. Suddenly, the butterflies began to fly around them, until the presence of the two became a blur; in that field of dreams they lost themselves in passion.

In time, it was dark with a full moon that would make any lover blush. Gabriel started a fire by the lake.

He and Rachel sat around the fire talking.

"Can I ask you a question, Gabriel?"

"Go for it."

"Where are we going with this relationship?"

"Well, I would like to think that it will last

Prelude to Dichotomy

forever. You would think that when two people love each other and everything feels right they deserve to be together no matter what. On the other hand, the right in me says that we need to walk away and never look back. But baby, I don't know how to let you go, you are so apart of me that it scares me.

Just to think there is a possibility that we have to walk away breaks my heart."

They sat.

"That night I stayed at your house, you asked me why didn't Robert and I have any kids...There's something I want to share with you, and please never share what I'm about to say with anyone," Rachel made him promise.

"The reason we don't have any kids is Robert can't have them".

"I'm so sorry," consoled Gabriel.

"It's been hard on him. I believe that's why he buries himself in his work to cover up the pain. So, you understand why I can't get pregnant, it would kill him; and knowing myself, I couldn't get an abortion. Do you see my dilemma?" She made another feeble attempt to

The Truth Be Known

do what was right.

"Yes baby, I do." Under the stars, Gabriel pulled Rachel to him and they both laid back reflecting. How ironic it was for him to be here with the one woman he retired his player card for, but couldn't have. Why had he let this happen? He knew his game; how to dodge the hook. With his own net, he fell into the love trap. While assuring her, he himself was not certain what would become of them. Even worse, for the first time, it scared him. He was afraid of the condition he would be left in if it ended now. Pain was inevitable either way they turned. This was unfamiliar territory.

The next morning Gabriel awoke to the smell of breakfast. He left the bedroom and approached Rachel at the kitchen counter with her head buried under folded arms, in anguish. She felt like she was running into a brick wall. Having tried many times to break away from him she couldn't let go. Also, she was running from truths in her marriage. She would never have children of her own; she had been starving for fulfillment past beauty and wealth at this stage

Prelude to Dichotomy

of her life; and her quest was purpose, but she kept coming up empty. Thinking there had to be more, she suspected children was the missing ingredient. Now awaited a boat to carry her off as soon as she was ready to sail. Robert managed to hold up to everything well; transitions, work pressures, disappointments and lately he was considering aspirations he had prepared years in college for. Whatever doubts and issues he may have had, he found a way to overcome them. She needed to find what was missing in her life, then maybe she could make things better…

"Rachel, what's wrong?" Gabriel asked.

"Robert is on his way. He wants to spend one day with me here at the cabin. Gabe, I'm torn in two," she answered crying. "I can't just turn my feelings on and off for my husband."

He took her in his arms. "Don't worry."

"You'd better be going, his plane is landing in ten minutes. It doesn't take him long to get here from the airport."

Gabriel kissed her and went back into the guest room to gather his things. As he walked out the front door, Rachel sat on the pool deck

The Truth Be Known

and tried to compose herself before her husband made his arrival.

Chapter Ten

Do The Seasons Change

The night was as glorious as they come for the holidays. Jack Frost made his presence known in the city of Memphis. The O'donalds hosted a Christmas party and everybody who was somebody would be there. There was a level of excitement in the air, being that Robert O'donald had thrown his name into the hat for candidacy of the mayoral race. He had the support of Senator Jamison who was a good friend of his family, and even Governor Gill saw the thirty-two year old man climbing the ranks quickly. If Entertainment Tonight was looking for an ideal expose', they should have made the affair. The beautiful estate lit up like the White House that evening and as for the band, its performance of

Prelude to Dichotomy

Christmas classics resonated like a Macy's parade.

Finally the couple of the hour glided down the stairway. The guests applauded at their striking appearance. There was no misunderstanding that evening who the lady of the castle was.

Mrs. O'donald looked as lovely as a painted portrait, dressed in a white chiffon evening gown, while displaying total grace and style. Searching through the crowd, she spotted Gabriel standing next to Lacy Bradley, Robert's assistant who was scheduled to be in Detroit.

Rachel inquired, "Baby, I thought you took Lacy to the airport earlier?"

"I invited her to the party. Our good friend Gabriel was in need of a companion and there was no way a friend of mine was going to be dateless on a night like this," said her husband with zest, caught up in the thrill of evening.

"You should have told me what you were planning," she was irritated.

"I really didn't think it was anything to ask you about," replied Robert, observing a reaction in her he was unused to, as they mingled in with the crowd.

Rachel made her way to the couple which now glided across the dance floor. As she stood looking like an eagle ready to attack its prey, Senator Jamison came up behind her.

"Tell me young lady, why isn't a beautiful lady like yourself on the dance floor?"

"Senator, I was just wondering the same thing, and do you know what?"

"No, what?" he answered gaily.

"You just saved me," Rachel said, thinking of his timely intervention.

"Then it sounds like I've done my civic duty."

"And you do it well," she expressed gratefully.

While the senator and Rachel danced, Gabriel walked up.

"Excuse me sir, may I cut in," he asked, while straightening his black bowtie.

"And who are you young man?"

"I'm Gabriel Armour, a good friend of the O'donalds."

The senator looked at Rachel protectively.

Prelude to Dichotomy

"Is this true young lady?"
"Yes sir."
"Well, I guess this old goose will fly."
"If it helps Senator, I did vote for you," Gabriel smiled.
"In that case, I don't feel so bad," laughed the senator who kissed Rachel's hand then walked off.
"May I have this dance?" Asked Gabriel.
Rachel looked at Gabriel, trying to decide between slapping him or kissing him.
"You looked like you were enjoying yourself with my husband's assistant."
Being that she was fully aware of his and Lacy's previous fling, he chose his words carefully,
"Are you asking me if I enjoyed her company?"
"No, I don't think I have to ask you that, I saw you were."
"You know, you're very beautiful when you're jealous," Gabriel teased.
"I don't find that amusing, sir."
"Why don't we just cherish the time we do

Do The Seasons Change

have."

"But I want so much more, Mr. Armour."

For a brief moment, their eyes locked and the inevitable happened. Rachel and Gabriel kissed. Suddenly, Rachel remembered herself and pulled back, but not quickly enough. Her husband stood over the shoulder of his good friend Gabriel with eyes filled with pain. Gabriel stood before Robert and dropped his head. Rachel dashed off the dance floor.

All had vacated the premises and there remained no evidence of the joyous celebration just hours before. Upstairs in their bedroom Robert sat on the floor while Rachel sat on the bed in complete silence. Robert broke the stillness.

"How long has it been going on?" He asked.

"What are you talking about?"

"So, you're going to deny that something is going on between you and Gabriel?"

"I'm so sorry Robert, I didn't plan for it to happen," she confessed.

Robert yelled at her, "How long, Rachel? You owe me at least that. My God, what was it? What else could you want? You have every-

Prelude to Dichotomy

thing a woman could ever ask for."

Rachel went to sit by Robert. She fell on him, weeping. "It wasn't you. I'm sorry I hurt you." Robert pushed her off and stood up. "I'm going to ask you one more da–," he stopped himself from cursing. It was not a normal practice. He'd always believed that a man was only as intelligent as the words he spoke, but tonight, it took everything in him to hold his tongue. "You make me sick." He picked up their wedding picture on the nightstand and threw it against the wall. Then he stormed out of the house.

Chapter Eleven

The Better Man

Back at home sitting outside on the snow filled deck, Gabriel mentally rewound the drama from earlier, when he heard a knock at his door.

"Are you going to invite me in?" Robert asked through the glass door.

"Come in," he answered rather apprehensively.

Robert walked in and headed toward the wine display. He poured himself a drink. Always trying to be a good man, and where did it get him! He was stoned.

"Since when did you start drinking?" Questioned Gabriel.

"Every since I found out my good pal has been knocking my wife."

Prelude to Dichotomy

Gabriel sat down on the sofa. "Doc, I'm sorry for what I've done."

Robert looked at Gabriel and shook his head.

"Maybe you'd like to tell me how long this little escapade has been going on?"

"What will it change, you knowing?"

"I think I have the right to know," Robert demanded. "When, where, and how long?"

Robert walked over and shoved Gabriel.

"Come on man, you're drunk. Don't be pushing on me".

As Gabriel turned to walk away, Robert hit him on one side of his jaw, knocking him to the floor.

"Just stay down there. If you get up, I might shoot you". Robert stood over Gabriel with his hand on his pistol. "You did me wrong, man, I trusted you. I'm warning you, stay away from my wife, or the next time I will pull the trigger."

Robert left Gabriel still in the floor.

The process of two months nearly destroyed Robert and Rachel's relationship. It felt like a knife piercing him through the heart everyday since that colder than winter evening; but, the O'donalds found grace with God, as He helped one wounded husband try to salvage what was left, and one wandering wife restore favor with her husband.

Rachel was in the shower when she felt sharp pains in her lower stomach. She turned the nozzle off, stepped out and went over to the mirror. Her stomach was protruding and her cycle was late; six weeks, to be exact. She knew when to expect her monthly and was seldom ever wrong.

Yet, she had allowed a few extra days before panicking. Sitting on her chaise, she began to pray.

"Lord, please don't let me be pregnant. My husband is just now able to be civil with me, please Jesus, help me."

At that moment she heard Robert coming into their bedroom. She quickly grabbed her bathrobe, covered herself and sat. He passed by her, obviously looking for something. He passed by her again and walked out, but not before kissing her this time.

"Good morning, baby," he said with his arms

Prelude to Dichotomy

around her waist.

She shifted nervously.

"There's something different with you, what is it?" He asked.

Rachel thought to say something that would take his attention off her stomach. "I've been working out…So my body is uh…kind of adjusting."

"Well, whatever you're doing, keep on doing it because it has you glowing. I like it."

Rachel turned to her husband and hugged him tightly.

"Is everything alright?"

"It's fine, you have a very good day," she assured him.

"I'm not going to be working late this evening, let's take the horses out. I know it's been a minute since we've had some fun, I'll even pack warm soup for the ride." Robert kissed his wife then left for the meeting with his campaign coordinator.

Rachel walked around in her denim jeans, breaking them in for the horse trail when she began to feel sick. Suddenly, she vomited uncontrollably all over everywhere and fell to the floor. She caught her breath long enough to make her way back up the stairs.

Robert arrived early as promised, to a pitch dark house. Calling her name, he strolled by doorways downstairs. When she didn't answer, he skipped the steps two at a time toward their bedroom. She wasn't there. He saw the bathroom light on and went in. She had been leaning over the toilet throwing up. He knelt beside her.

"Baby, what's going on with you?"

"I'm not doing so well, she said.

"Do you know what's wrong?"

She nodded yes with her head still in the bowl.

Robert spotted a home pregnancy test beside her. He stood up and asked dryly, "So, do I need to ask the result, or am I looking at it?"

Rachel pulled her head out of the toilet. "I'm so sorry," she said, lying her weary head on the toilet seat.

He walked over to the sink to grab a towel, wet it and sat next to his wife. Taking her into his arms, he began to wipe her face with the cool,

Prelude to Dichotomy

thick cloth.

"Does he know?"

Rachel shook her head no.

"Are you going to tell him?"

"No", she answered.

"Alright, there's only one thing to do; I'm going to drop out of the race."

"Robert, no. I'm not going to let you. You've worked too hard for this."

"I'd rather bow out now, before it turns into a fiasco for the five O'clock news," he imagined the scrutiny, "no, it's settled, I'm going to be needed at home more with my wife and baby." He helped Rachel over to the sink, then lifted her up in his arms to carry her to their bed where she fell fast asleep.

The next morning Rachel awoke to her spouse overlooking the balcony. She called him to the bed and he responded by lying next to her.

"Is everything alright?" He asked caringly.

"Yes, I was just wondering what was on your mind.

Robert, be honest with me, how do you feel about me being pregnant?"

The Better Man

Robert turned away to hide the emotion displayed in his eyes; then Rachel's slender fingers pulled his face to hers so she could see them.

"You know more than anything I wanted to give you that one thing," her husband cleared his throat and paused to pull himself together. In the nine years they had been married, she had always seen him strong. "I've been able to give you any material thing your heart desired but the one thing that mattered most, I feel I've failed you."

Rachel pulled Robert to her breasts where he lied his head. "My husband, you didn't fail me, I failed you; and I don't know how to undo what I've done." Her voice began to crack. "Robert, if you want me to have an abortion, I will."

"Rachel, a part of me wants you to have an abortion, but, there's another part that says you shouldn't have to suffer for my inability. I was asking God this morning, why me? I've always tried to do people right. Then, something occurred to me, things happen for a reason. So, to answer your question Rachel, no. We're going keep the baby and I will love him like my very

Prelude to Dichotomy

own," he smiled hopefully.

Chapter Twelve

Playing With My Mind

A new and older assistant met with Gabriel who replaced Lacy on the O'donald project. Gabriel curiously wondered who had arranged the change, but didn't dare ask Mr. Davis. Instead, he expediently briefed Ms. Lee on the account and they plunged into the task.

"So, you're the famous Mr. Armour," she said, almost too anxiously, when they finally stopped working.

It seemed his reputation among the women had started to spread into the professional arena.

"Is that a good thing or a bad thing?" He was almost too afraid to ask.

"I've heard nothing but good things about your work."

Prelude to Dichotomy

"By Mrs. O' donald?" Replied Gabriel, trying to sound casual in mentioning Rachel's name.

"On the contrary," she said. "By Mr. O'donald himself."

He hesitated. "So, how are The O'donalds?"

"They're doing well. You know they're expecting a baby?"

Gabriel sat up straight in his seat, as usual when things caught his attention.

"No, I didn't know. How many months is she?" He asked cautiously.

"The baby is due any day now."

"And how's Mrs. O'donald handling her pregnancy?" He probed further.

"I've never seen a pregnant woman as radiant as she. She looks like a doll," rattled the unsuspecting Ms. Lee who now turned to glance at her watch and recalled another appointment for across town. Gabriel expressed how good it was to meet her and that he looked forward to seeing her next time.

It was a wow! time in Memphis. The park was packed like a can of sardines with mixed

Playing With My Mind

faces enjoying food and fun, while the merry hearts of children awaited nightfall for the firework spectaculars. Gabriel and Amy, his date, strolled riverfront on July fourth and followed the flavorful smell of Oriental food. Amy saw a "China Inn Express" booth and stated she'd heard a lot about the restaurant and wanted to see if it lived up to its reputation. Gabriel cautiously searched the vender area for a familiar face and saw Robert.

He lied to Amy. "Take this money, get whatever you want and I'll have whatever you're having.

I need to go to the men's quarters." They agreed to meet back at their seats later. Walking toward the porter stalls, he ran into Rachel.

How good she looked to him. She must have been the most beautiful pregnant woman he had ever seen. Her skin was like undiminished gold as it glowed in the sunlight, perspiring in the heat of mid summer. Her hair was as glorious as it was long under a cap advertising the phrase "Best China in Town." There, coming out of the porter potty and wiping her hands, he walked up

Prelude to Dichotomy

behind her.

"Hello Rachel."

She turned around, not very surprised to see him.

"How have you been?" He asked.

"I've been pregnant and well," she laughed lightly.

"I think you look lovely," he said softly.

"Thank you," she answered in low key.

"Do you know what you're having?"

Rachel put one hand on her stomach, "She's a girl."

Gabriel dropped his head, near speechless, then looked at her.

"Do you have a name picked out?" He asked.

"We're thinking about Nattily."

"I like that name, it's different."

"Thank you," she answered, even more softly.

Now, the words between Gabriel and Rachel were few, but their eyes said what they dared not utter.

"Well, it was good seeing you again," Rachel

Playing With My Mind

said.

"You too," he replied.

She began to walk away and Gabriel called her.

"Yes," she stopped.

"If you need anything, will you let me know?" He said.

Rachel nodded then vanished into the crowd.

Gabriel finally made his way back to his seat where his date had been waiting.

"Hey stranger, I thought you got lost."

"I apologize, I ran into an old friend."

"By your expression, it doesn't look like good news."

Gabriel took a deep breath and sighed, "Let's just say I wish things were better."

Amy leaned over and whispered into Gabriel ear, "How about if we go back to your house and I'll give you a massage and a little lam yap."

He sat up, "What's lam yap?"

"It means, a little something extra."

He laughed. "That lam yap sounds nice, but truthfully, I don't think I'm going to be good

Prelude to Dichotomy

company tonight."

"Are you going to leave me?"

"I hope you wont hold it against me, I promise I'll make it up to you 'double fold' like the preachers say."

"Well in that case, I'll relieve you of your duties," she stated understandably.

Gabriel and Amy leaned in and kissed, then he stood and walked up to his place on the river. As he slowly walked through the crowd, he glanced over at the food stand to see Rachel listening to the orchestra. He desperately wanted the woman he loved to look his way, but he was no more than a speck in the multitude of people now. Gabriel finally realized why Robert was so in love.

His wife was truly something special. She was a beautiful woman and sought to do what was proper. She was a sharp business partner and a fun companion. She was someone to be cherished.

That evening Robert and Rachel were so tired, they left some of their equipment in the hauling van. He was knocked out, while her

Playing With My Mind

mind drifted in the early hours.

She spoke silently, "Dear God, I pray that you will hear me. I know you haven't heard from me in a long while, but I need your help. I have messed up badly. You know my situation, I'm carrying another man's baby and my heart is somewhere between home and longing to be with the father of my child. Can you give me an answer? Please take this pain away that's been here too long."

Her husband was dressed and ready for the airport a couple hours later. He leaned down and kissed her.

"Baby, wake up."
"What time is it?" She asked disoriented.
"It's six-thirty."
"Are you going to be alright by yourself?"
"I'll be fine," she assured him, sending her regards to their work associates in the North.

Robert looked carefully at his wife, then walked into their room to grab his luggage, heading for Detroit.

At about eight-thirty that same morning, Gabriel was shaving when he heard someone

Prelude to Dichotomy

knocking at his front door. Through the glass, he saw Rachel.

"Can I come in?"

"Please do."

He shut the door behind her, wiping off the last of his musk scented shaving cream. "What brings you to my neighborhood?"

"I probably shouldn't be here." She reached for the doorknob to leave when Gabriel grabbed her arm.

"Please don't."

She turned and looked at him. "I got up, heading for my morning walk and somehow I've ended up here, I know I shouldn't be here."

"Whether you're supposed to be here or not is irrelevant, you're here now. I've really missed you, lady."

"This is hard for me Gabriel, I'm so confused."

Gabriel held her in his arms, then took her by her small wrists into the kitchen and whipped up a hefty breakfast; pancakes, bacon, eggs, grits and a tall glass of freshly squeezed orange juice.

"So have you prepared the baby room?"

Playing With My Mind

"Yes, it's pink, very pink."
Gabriel laughed.
"What's so funny said Rachel?
"You really like pink."
"I believe every girl should be feminine and her room should reflect that."
"Well, my sister had a blue bedroom."
Rachel laughed, "That's a boy's color, a girl should have a girly room."
"So, when she becomes a woman, what should the color of her room be?" Asked Gabriel.
"Then she should choose according to her personality or whatever fits her skin tone."
Gabriel smiled at her, "You actually sound like you know what you're talking about."
"Don't play, one thing I can do is dress," Rachel defended.
They both laughed and laughed until they forgot all about their anxieties. Soon, the time came that neither of them wanted to see. She had to go to a business meeting and Gabriel had to be in at ten O'clock.
"I wish today was the weekend, that's when

Prelude to Dichotomy

time doesn't matter," said Gabriel.

Gabriel and Rachel looked at one another. He saw farewell in her eyes as she reached out her hands to him. He grabbed her fingers and intertwined them.

"I'm leaving," she spoke softly.

"What are you talking about?" He answered.

"We're moving to Detroit. We need a new start and the business is profitable there."

Gabriel was quiet. Then the man of steel cried.

Rachel knelt in front of him, held him and let him know that it would be okay. Their paths had crossed for a reason and though they would no longer be together, they would share one thing, an incredible moment in time. At the front door, they embraced.

At that magical moment, she felt her stomach jump. Gabriel put his hand on her stomach and smiled as tears ran down both their faces. He knelt down, pulled Rachel's shirt up and kissed her round belly. Letting her go, he watched until he could no longer see her or his baby.

Playing With My Mind

They had well planned the trip and by that weekend the city of Memphis was already behind the O'donalds, as their new family traveled Northward.

Chapter Thirteen

Hello Again

Five years passed and Gabriel's life was back on track. He had rekindled a few old flames and lit a couple of new ones. He was still quite the ladies' man with one exception, he wasn't trying to break all the women's hearts these days, just one or two every now and then, to be sure he still had the touch. One beautiful Spring day, Gabriel was in his office when Mr. Davis entered quietly and sat on the sofa.

"What's wrong Mr. D., what's on your mind?"

"Son, you might want to have a seat."

Gabriel followed his advice.

"I just got off of the phone with Rachel. She and her family are moving back to Memphis.

Prelude to Dichotomy

Their daughter has a serious medical condition and they have admitted her into the children's hospital. From the way it sounds, it doesn't look well."

"Did she say what was wrong with her?" Gabriel felt his heart sink.

"The child was born with deteriorating heart disease; only thirty percent is functional and it is constantly weakening."

"Mr. D., there's so much I would like to tell you, but I can't," Gabriel admitted.

"One of the benefits of a God parent is knowing things about a child that his parents don't and getting to play the cool card. You don't have to say a thing, I know and have known a long time," said the man thirty-five years his senior. "Rachel asked me not to say anything, but I think this is an opportunity to right a wrong; this is just as much as your problem as hers. By the way, the baby is on the fourth floor and you didn't hear it from me."

Gabriel nodded, letting Mr. D. know that he understood what he was saying.

That night Gabriel couldn't sleep. He got

Hello Again

up to fix himself a drink and stood at his wet bar thinking about the child who didn't ask to come into this world, but was brought here by two people's selfish desires. He angrily hit the wall bruising his knuckles, then went back into his bedroom and put on some slacks and a shirt.

When Gabriel arrived at the hospital, he passed the security guard and walked up to the front desk, requesting his daughter's room number.

"Sir, you do know that visiting hours are over."

"I didn't know", he replied.

"If you come back tomorrow, you can see her."

Gabriel looked at the nurse for a long moment, "Yes ma'am, thank you for your help." Walking away, he slowly glanced back to assure that no one was looking, then took flight up the stairs to the fourth floor. He walked toward the door but became paralyzed momentarily, suddenly realizing he did not know what to say to the child; but then forced the door open. The golden toned girl was lying in a bed hooked up

Prelude to Dichotomy

to a breathing machine. So lovely, she was the essence of her mother, with slanted, brown eyes. Gabriel walked over to her, noticing a portrait of her happy family that was pinned to a bulletin board. He laid his hand on the young child's face and brushed her soft cheeks.

A familiar voice from behind greeted him.

"She's very precious," answered Gabriel.

"Yes she is," said Rachel.

Gabriel now turned to face the child's mother." "How have you been, lady?"

"Gabriel, I'm tired, I can't take seeing my baby like this."

"Is there anything I can do?"

"No, she has the best nurses and Robert's taken care of everything else. She's his little Angel."

"I can imagine," he replied, looking for Robert to enter the room any minute.

"He's meeting with the buyer of our home, he won't be here until Sunday."

"Do you still have the cabin?" Gabriel remembered that special day.

"Yes, that's one property I can't bring myself

Hello Again

to sell."

They stepped away to talk, walking into the cafeteria.

"What are they doing to remedy the problem?" Gabriel asked.

"They're saying she's going to need a heart transplant, her health is rapidly declining."

"So, can we get her another heart?"

"It's not that easy, she's on a waiting list and it has to be the proper match, then she can have the surgery."

A few minutes later they were back into Nattily's room where Rachel sat at the foot of the bed and Gabriel stood by Nattily's side. As he stroked her wavy black hair, Nattily awakened.

"Are you my doctor?" The girl asked faintly.

"No, little lady, I'm a friend of your mom and dad."

Nattily saw her mother, "Mommy, I want my daddy."

Rachel stood beside her. Taking her hand, she comforted her, "He'll be here in two days and he told me to tell you that he's bringing you something special."

Prelude to Dichotomy

Nattily smiled largely as she attempted to grasp air. "Mommy, why is that man crying?"

Rachel glanced at Gabriel, "Baby, his tears are called happy tears, he's glad to see you," she whispered, while Gabriel thought sadly about how he had missed so many wonderful days of his daughter's life.

The first night Gabriel met his daughter, he couldn't bring himself to leave her side. He wanted to take in as much of her as possible, being he only had a couple of days to get to know her. In the short time, Nattily had grown attached to his funny faces and blew him joyful kisses. He thanked Rachel for allowing him to experience some of the most meaningful days of his life, then turned one last time to the little girl and kissed her tender cheeks. Tears of love dropped from his eyes to her face. He took out a handkerchief to wipe her tears and gave it to her to keep. Finally, he stepped out of the room and waited for Rachel to join him. As he stood by the door, he heard Nattily describe a dream she had to her mother.

"Mommy, I saw an Angel in my dreams."

Hello Again

"You did? Well, what did the Angel say, sweety?"

"He said the man who was just in my room was my daddy; and the Angel is coming to take me away, but he told me to tell you everything is going to work out well."

Rachel listened quietly and smiled as tears streamed down her face. Gabriel cried too and left to go home.

Now in his bed, he fell asleep in a fetal position. He was still sleep that night at eleven when his phone rang. Nat had turned for the worst. Rachel invited him to see their daughter once again before Robert arrived. He jumped out of bed with his heart racing.

Nat was unconscious and unresponsive this time. Pulling her fragile body to him, he held her as she was sound asleep.

Ending Prologue

It's Saturday morning and usually my favorite time of year, but being chauffeured to my daughter's funeral on this twenty-fifth day of March has a way of changing my perspective.

She wasn't even five years old. When I saw her lying there helplessly during the service, I wanted to pick her up and blow life into her fragile body.

Now looking out of the limo window, I sit amazed at God's many creations: I see birds flying across the vast blue sky, squirrels jumping from tree to tree, and I dare mention the beautiful pastel flowers gracing the earth with all their splendor. Yet, there are no birds soaring in my heart nor flowers watering the pain of my soul; bitterness alone overwhelms me.

Since God is taking care of all the birds, trees, and

Prelude to Dichotomy

billions of His other creatures, why couldn't he save Nat? He should have taken my life. Children are supposed to bury their parents, not parents bury their children.

Chapter Fourteen

Make It Stop!

One whole month dragged by since his daughter's death and Gabriel decided to go from a social drinker to becoming a public drunk.

It was a Monday morning and Gabriel's alarm clock sounded. He sat up on the edge of his bed and reached over to shut the clock up. He was met by a friendly smile from a bottle of E&J on the night stand. He opened it and went from one sip, to another, drinking the whole bottle. After finishing the bottle, he went to the commode. Sighting his reflection in the mirror, he was angered at the thought of still being alive. Sunday night he drank enough to make any normal human being's heart stop.

Gabriel Armour arrived at his office hours

Prelude to Dichotomy

late on the second day of the week and greeted everyone he saw unashamedly drunk, including his boss.

"Would you like to talk, son?"

"No, I'm good, Mr. D."

"It looks like you're trying to get yourself fired, which may well be deserved, but I am not going to fire you, Gabriel. I am going to give you another chance. I want you to take six weeks off with the understanding that when you return, you're going to have yourself together."

Gabriel thanked Mr. Davis and apologized for his actions as soberly as he could. The boss further called down to the mailroom for Elmo to assist his intoxicated friend in his transit home. Gabriel saluted Elmo after he stumbled out of the car and went inside to finish off the other half bottle of his day's courage.

Within seconds he heard a doorbell ring.

"Yes, may I help you?" Asked Gabriel.

"Hello, I'm the pastor of Christian Vision Center, the church up the street and I would like to invite you to our Sunday service."

Gabriel looked at the pastor, and started

Make It Stop!

laughing. "I don't mean to be a donkey, but me and God aren't on speaking terms."

"If you don't mind me asking, was it a divorce?"

"Preacher man, I don't do therapy sessions at my front door, and especially with people I don't know."

"I can respect that," answered Pastor Chiles.

"Can I leave you with a little information about my church?"

"No problem", said Gabriel, who took the pamphlets then shut the door.

Unable to get back to sleep, Gabriel freshened up and decided to go out for something to eat but realized his car was still at the office. So, he walked up the street to the Gentleman's Club to get a bite to eat. He was met at the lounge door by two lovely young women sporting the latest designers by mother nature. They led him to a booth in the back.

"Would you like some company?" Asked one.

"Certainly. Would it be a problem if both of you took a seat?"

Prelude to Dichotomy

"Not at all," said one of the hostesses.

While one young lady entertained Gabriel, the red head went and found his pleasure from the food menu; then she fed him and wiped his mouth. He was feeling very comfortable now. After they talked awhile, it seemed they made a type of chemical connection.

"So, what would a person have to do to get what we have going on to last a little longer?"

"Name the place and the time and we'll see what we can do."

Gabriel grabbed a napkin from off the table and wrote his address down. "So, how much damage is it going to be?"

"It will be three hundred dollars; before the entertainment starts we want our money," said the young lady.

"I can handle that," agreed Gabriel, as he grinned with anticipation. He made his way back home to get ready for the next rumble. Eager at the knock of his front door and ready for the freak show to begin, he opened it with a welcoming smile.

"And hello—" he said. His smile immediately

Make It Stop!

turned into a frown.

"I thought you liked me," said the preacher, laughing at his expression.

"Sorry Rev, I don't mean to be rude, the smile wasn't for you, but for the two freaks I'm expecting."

"I came at the right time," the pastor said humorously, "we can have prayer, amen!"

"Wrong! There's not going to be any prayer going on in this house tonight, preacher," declared Gabriel.

"Well, I came back to your door because God told me to bring you this book which was in my bookstore."

Gabriel knew little about God. "Man, have you been smoking?"

"No…God still is in the talking business. He also wanted me to tell you that he loves you very much."

Gabriel looked down for a brief moment, "Thank you, preacher."

Pastor Chiles saw the two women pulling up in a red sports sedan.

"Would those be the ladies you're waiting

Prelude to Dichotomy

for?"

"That's them," said Gabriel.

"Before I leave, may I pray for you?"

"Only if it's quick," said an anxious Gabriel.

Pastor Chiles bowed his head, "My father God, I thank you for this young man. Lord, I pray three things for him; that you will resurrect him, restore him, and use him for your glory. Let him know, Daddy, that the bottle—I mean the battle isn't his, but the Lord's, in Jesus Christ's name, amen."

Gabriel and the pastor shook hands, then the pastor walked away and nodded at the young women.

Now at Gabriel's house the party began with them on the couch talking and drinking, then one thing lead to another. One girl danced out of her clothes while the other undressed Gabriel down to nothing, until every imaginably sleaky-freaky fantasy he could conceive was satisfied.

The next morning Gabriel awakened to an empty bed; the two women he entertained had let themselves out. In the front room was three hundred dollars still sitting on his wet bar with

Make It Stop!

a note attached to it.

"Gabriel, Spice and I enjoyed ourselves. This time was on us...But next time–you know the bizz.

Keep in touch. Sincerely, Goldfingers."

Gabriel laughed as he thought to himself that she gained her stripper name rightfully so, but he would call her "Hypnotic" because she had him in the clouds all night long.

The two months allowance for bereavement proved to be wasted time on Gabriel's carousing and prodigal living. He did manage to check in on the work crew once, during which time Mr. D. offered him advice...Something about sexual caution and the company he'd been keeping. Gabriel wasn't trying to hear it though. He was too numb to be taking notes these days. The pain and sorrow of his lost was almost unbearable now, which he admitted to Mr. D., along with the discovery that he wasn't Superman–even he wasn't that shatterproof.

All of the bad seed Gabriel now recalled planting seemed to be coming up in one big heap. Pain seeded had a way of coming back to heart-

Prelude to Dichotomy

felt hurt; and it seemed to be following him everywhere. One day, he walked around the men's clothing store and heard a little girl's giggle coming from the racks, then saw her little face peaking out at him. She smiled and disappeared into the suits. He looked around to see where her parents were and realized she was playing hide-and-seek with her father. Gabriel was so overwhelmed by the scene that he quickly left the store. Not looking for any particular place but just trying to clear his head, he walked the blocks of downtown, leaving his freshly waxed BMW on the parking lot.

March twenty-fifth ...He marked the three events in his life which ironically took place on that same day. One, the first night he slept with Sheila Anderson, nearly seven years ago. Two, the day he received a subpoena to the courthouse concerning her, which was a year later. He recalled how she tried to make him pay half the doctor bills for her complications; but his strong persuasion convinced her to have an abortion, which incidentally, cleared his case. Three, the day of Nattily's funeral.

Make It Stop!

In conclusion, Gabriel blamed God for all his pain. Apparently, the Man Upstairs was an excellent scorekeeper of all misuse of females and strike three meant Gabriel was out.

Finding himself in front of a corner church with a sign on it which read, "Christian Vision Center,

Pastor Chiles," the bitter black male felt the urge to go in and give this pastor a piece of his mind; to warn him to stay away from his house. He went into The House of God, took a seat on the back row and mentally rehearsed his unholy speech.

The preacher was at the altar praying in a foreign language. Trying to figure out what it was, Gabriel was unfamiliar with the dialect and suspected it was probably some type of Bible code for crooked preachers.

He waited and listened for every bit of fifteen minutes; not once did the pastor look up to see who had come into the sanctuary. Finally, Gabriel got up to leave. At the same time, the pastor stopped speaking in the peculiar tongue and spoke clearly in English, "The Lord God

Prelude to Dichotomy

saith—"

Gabriel turned to see who else was in the sanctuary, but it was only he and the pastor.

"—She's with him, and you're not to worry. All will work out well, it's for your good." Then the preacher went back to speaking in the unknown tongue. Gabriel thought to himself how mysterious it was that the pastor said the same thing he heard his four-year-old daughter tell her mother; and even stranger, the man's eyes had never opened to see who was in the building. He left out of the church quickly, more confused now than before he went in.

Rachel called to check on her astray friend that day. She said she'd been sleeping a lot lately and had lost a lot of weight since he saw her at the funeral. He longed to hold her and stroke her soft hair, but oddly, Gabriel advised that she take care of Robert because her husband also needed her. She consented and thanked him for the love he showed to her and Nattily. She laid the phone down and promised herself again never to call her deeply felt fortress of love.

Chapter Fifteen

Only You, Lord

Since he last talked with Rachel it had been weeks, and when Gabriel found himself yearning for female companionship, he decided to invite Hypnotic back over along with her sidekick. The duo lived up to his expectations of making a brother weak at his knees. Somewhere between telling the women to "show out" and watching them from a blurry distance, he passed out totally.

He was awakened by the sound of a loud pop, like a gunshot. Gabriel jumped up. Looking around at his surroundings which were unfamiliar, he stood in a courtroom shackled from arms to feet with two oversized men standing beside him. When trying to speak to one of

Prelude to Dichotomy

the men, his voice was silenced in this unknown world. A man in a robe pointed at him. Hardly making out the words, Gabriel read the lips of the man in the chair.

"...He will be eternally cursed for not believing in the Father, not accepting the Son, and not fellowshipping with the Holy Spirit. Depart from me, for I do not know you. Gabriel Deshez Armour, I sentence you to the lake of hell..." Suddenly, the two men grabbed him and took him to a large door which opened itself. Gabriel saw fire and they pushed him into it.

Opening his mouth in panic and jumping forward, he realized it was only a bad dream. Visibly shaking by the scene, he lied back in relief. He was a really bad boy, last night, he remembered. It must have been his conscious warning him.

His cell phone startled him. "Hello."

"I'm sorry to be calling you with bad news, but Rachel is in the hospital."

"What's wrong with her?"

"She tried to commit suicide. It was prescription pills—"

Only You, Lord

Something about this scene was all too familiar by now to Gabriel, as he hurried to the hospital. He couldn't remember if he had hung up the phone after talking with Mr. D. or not.

Robert was talking with the doctor in the lobby of Rachel's ward, when Gabriel arrived. "What are you doing here?"

"I'm just checking on her, is she alright?"

"She's fine," said the protective husband. If his wife was dying, it would be his eyes she looked into last, not this punk loverboy. Mr. Robert O'donald believed he had earned every honorable right.

Gabriel followed him, "Robert, I know you don't want me here, but I need to see her."

"If you don't leave, I'm going to call security, and if they can't get you to leave, it's not going to be nice up in here–now go."

Not wanting to cause the family more sorrow, Gabriel left.

Standing in front of his penthouse in the pouring rain, Gabriel broke down. He dropped to the ground and wept despairingly; then lifted his face toward Heaven and cursed God for all

Prelude to Dichotomy

that He put him through. No longer caring whether he lived or died, he decided he was better off dead and determined to kill himself the moment he reached the other side of his front door. He mentally pictured himself pulling his nine millimeter trigger to his head. A flicker of optimism wished that there was a God who cared enough about him to give Gabriel one reason to change his mind before he walked inside.

"Mr. Armour, are you alright?" He heard a voice.

Gabriel looked up and began to laugh at the sight of Pastor Chiles.

"You want to let me in on what's so funny about you lying on the ground in the rain?" Asked the preacher.

"God is a joke," Gabriel said sarcastically. "I asked Him if he was real to show me, and here you are to put another Bible pamphlet on my door."

In the rainstorm, Pastor Chiles set his umbrella down and knelt by Gabriel. "Young man, you have it all wrong; I was on my way to dinner with my wife when God spoke to me and told

Only You, Lord

me to come by and check on you. Mr. Armour, God sent me to let you know that He's concerned about you and that He loves you. He is calling you for a kingdom work."

Gabriel looked doubtfully at the preacher, "I've done so much wrong in my life, how can God forgive me?"

"Son, that's the good thing about it, Jesus Christ went to the cross for all of our sins; there's nothing you can ever do to make God stop loving you. God's not trying to take life from you, He's trying to get life to you. The Bible says in Romans ten and nine, that if you confess Jesus as your Lord and Savior, and you believe that He died on the cross, rose from the grave and is the Son of God, you will be saved."

"You mean that's all I have to do to go to Heaven and see my daughter again?"

Pastor Chiles nodded yes.

"Preacher, I want to be saved."

Pastor Chiles smiled at Gabriel. "To know God for yourself, repeat after me. Father God, I come to you the only way I know..."

Gabriel followed, "I thank you for forgiving

Prelude to Dichotomy

me for all my committed sins; I believe that your blood is strong enough to cleanse me. The Bible says that you are a faithful and a just God to wipe away my sins, so here they are and here I am. I believe what your Word says and today I am saved," in Jesus Christ's name, amen."

"Son, you are saved," said Pastor Chiles happily.

"So, if I died tonight I would go to Heaven?"

The preacher looked at him and nodded yes, "Just let that be of natural causes."

Gabriel leaped up. "Preacher, I know you must be a man of God for you to stand in this rain and tell me about your God. This Jesus must be the real deal. Thank you. Thank you for not giving up on me." Gabriel, the man's man, hugged the minister so tightly that he could have broken his ribs then took off running down the street. "I'll see you Sunday morning Rev."

Pastor Chiles waved at him and afterward thanked God for being so faithful; because he had been calling Gabriel's name in his prayers everyday.

Gabriel went back to the hospital in soaking

Only You, Lord

wet clothes to see Rachel. He prayed for her that she would be saved as he had been and healed, and he knew in his heart that from that day they would be no more as they were; as for him, it was time to do the will of his newly found God.

Thank You for Reading this Book.
We Hope You Enjoyed the Contents of its Pages.
Sincerely Yours,
Swan Publishing

LaVergne, TN USA
09 April 2010
178734LV00001B/5/P